ASTERIX IN SWITZERLAND

TEXT BY GOSCINNY

DRAWINGS BY UDERZO

TRANSLATED BY ANTHEA BELL AND DEREK HOCKRIDGE

Hodder
Children's
Books

a division of Hodder Headline plc

Asterix in Switzerland

Copyright © Dargaud Editeur 1970, Goscinny-Uderzo
English language text copyright © Brockhampton Press Ltd 1973

First published in Great Britain 1973 (cased)
by Hodder Dargaud Ltd
This edition first published 1976 by Knight Books, Hodder Dargaud

This impression: 1995 1996 1997 1998

ISBN 0 340 20942 9

Published by Hodder Dargaud Ltd,
338 Euston Road, London NW1 3BH

Printed in Belgium by Proost International Book Production

The year is 50 BC. Gaul is entirely occupied by the Romans. Well, not entirely... One small village of indomitable Gauls still holds out against the invaders. And life is not easy for the Roman legionaries who garrison the fortified camps of Totorum, Aquarium, Laudanum and Compendium...

a few of the Gauls

Asterix, the hero of these adventures. A shrewd, cunning little warrior; all perilous missions are immediately entrusted to him. Asterix gets his superhuman strength from the magic potion brewed by the druid Getafix...

Obelix, Asterix's inseparable friend. A menhir delivery-man by trade; addicted to wild boar. Obelix is always ready to drop everything and go off on a new adventure with Asterix — so long as there's wild boar to eat, and plenty of fighting.

Getafix, the venerable village druid. Gathers mistletoe and brews magic potions. His speciality is the potion which gives the drinker superhuman strength. But Getafix also has other recipes up his sleeve...

Cacofonix, the bard. Opinion is divided as to his musical gifts. Cacofonix thinks he's a genius. Everyone else thinks he's unspeakable. But so long as he doesn't speak, let alone sing, everybody likes him...

Finally, Vitalstatistix, the chief of the tribe. Majestic, brave and hot-tempered, the old warrior is respected by his men and feared by his enemies. Vitalstatistix himself has only one fear; he is afraid the sky may fall on his head tomorrow. But as he always says, 'Tomorrow never comes.'

BUT, CHIEF VITALSTATISTIX...

NO ARGUING! TO WORK!

TEEHEEHEE! YOU'D DO BETTER IF YOU WERE WALKING ALONG A SLOPE!

IT SHOWS THE CHIEF IS BENT ON GETTING A GOOD ANGLE ON THINGS!

PROVES WHAT YOU CAN DO IF YOU'VE GOT THE INCLINATION!

PUT ME DOWN, BOYS. I HAVE A SUSPICION THAT PEOPLE ARE LAUGHING AT US!

IT WOULD WORK BETTER IF OBELIX CARRIED YOU ON HIS OWN, O CHIEF

ON HIS OWN? IN HIS FULL CAPACITY, A CHIEF MUST BE SERVED BY TWO WARRIORS. I'D FEEL LIKE A HALF-PINT CHIEF IF...

ANYWAY, I'VE GOT SOME MENHIRS TO POLISH

SOON AFTERWARDS...

WHAT ON EARTH IS OBELIX DOING?

HE'S JUST SERVING A HALF-PINT OF MILD AND BITTER

BY TOUTATIS! ARE YOU REFUSING TO SERVE ME? I'M A MILD MAN, BUT THIS MAKES ME FEEL VERY BITTER!

THE GOOD HUMOUR PREVALENT IN THE GAULISH VILLAGE IS CONSPICUOUSLY ABSENT FROM THE PALACE OF VARIUS FLAVUS, THE POWERFUL ROMAN GOVERNOR OF CONDATUM *, THOUGH HIS GUESTS ARE DOING THEIR BEST TO HAVE A GOOD TIME...

* RENNES

BY JUPITER, O SUBLIME FLAVUS, YOUR ORGIES ARE BEAUTIFULLY DECADENT. THEY MAKE US QUITE FORGET HOW FAR WE ARE FROM ROME!

GOOD TASTE, THAT'S THE WHOLE SECRET... I GET THE ROMAN IMPRESARIO FELLINUS TO LAY ON MY ORGIES

BRING ON THE DANCING GIRLS!

ZING! BOOM! ZING! BOOM BOOM!

WINE! MORE WINE!

MASTER... THE PERSON YOU WERE EXPECTING IS IN YOUR ROOMS

COMING... BRING ON THE BOAR'S TRIPE FRIED IN AUROCHS DRIPPING!

YOU REALLY ARE SPOILING US, DIVINE FLAVUS!

HAVE FUN, FRIENDS! I'LL BE BACK IN A MINUTE

HAVEN'T YOU GOT YOUR GREEN BLUSHER? I WANT TO MAKE MYSELF LOOK WORSE

HI! SLAVE! THIS DISH IS CLEAN! IT'S DISGRACEFUL!

THAT'S RIGHT! WHY NOT FINGER-BOWLS, WHILE YOU'RE ABOUT IT?

9

HERE'S THE SOUP!

YOU MAKE YOURSELF PRETTY COMFORTABLE HERE... ODD, FOR THE GOVERNOR OF A PROVINCE SO POOR THAT IT CONTRIBUTES ONLY A FEW PIECES OF GOLD TO THE ROMAN TREASURY

GOOD TASTE, THAT'S THE SECRET. IT'S SURPRISING WHAT A LOT YOU CAN DO ON VERY LITTLE...

WELL, WE'LL SEE ABOUT THAT TOMORROW

GOOD NIGHT, QUAESTOR

TEE HEE HEE!

AND THAT NIGHT...

MASTER! MASTER! THE QUAESTOR'S BEEN TAKEN ILL

WHAT, ALREADY?

OOOOH! I FEEL TERRIBLE! I DON'T THINK I'LL LIVE, BY JUPITER!

IT MUST HAVE BEEN THE VEGETABLE SOUP. VERY INDIGESTIBLE. I'LL HAVE THE COOK WHIPPED

LEAVE THE COOK ALONE! SEND FOR DOCTORS INSTEAD!

GOOD IDEA! I'LL CALL IN ALL THE DOCTORS IN THE GARRISON.

AREN'T YOU AFRAID THE DOCTORS MAY SPOIL YOUR PLAN, O VARIUS FLAVUS?

I KNOW THE DOCTORS IN THIS GARRISON...

WHEN THEY GET TOGETHER, THEY'RE MORE MURDEROUS THAN A LEGION ARMED TO THE TEETH!

LATER THAT NIGHT...

THE DOCTORS ARE HERE, QUAESTOR...CAN THEY COME IN?

YES... OUCH!*

WHERE'S THE PATIENT?

IS HE THE ONE IN BED?

LEAVE HIM TO ME!

DON'T PUSH!

LET'S FEEL HIS PULSE!

HE'S IN CONVULSIONS

MY DEAR COLLEAGUE, I SHOULD SAY, MYSELF, THAT HE HAD PINS AND NEEDLES

YOU MUST BE JOKING, MY DEAR FELLOW! HE'S FEVERISH!

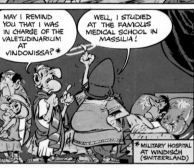

MAY I REMIND YOU THAT I WAS IN CHARGE OF THE VALETUDINARIUM AT VINDONISSA?*

WELL, I STUDIED AT THE FAMOUS MEDICAL SCHOOL IN MASSILIA!

* MILITARY HOSPITAL AT WINDISCH (SWITZERLAND)

CONSIDERING YOUR UGLY MUG, YOU OUGHT TO CONFINE YOUR ATTENTIONS TO STUDENT ORGIES!

MAYBE, BUT THE CASUALTIES IN THE VALETUDINARIUM AT VINDONISSA ARE A LOT HIGHER THAN IN ANY OF CAESAR'S CAMPAIGNS!

OOOOOOH!

WE MUST BLEED HIM!

HIS ARTERIES NEED AIR! WE'D BETTER BLOW SOME INTO HIM!

WHERE ARE THE CUCURBITULAE?*

YOU DON'T KNOW A THING! MIX UP SOME GROUND IVORY WITH TORTOISE AND PIGEON BLOOD! IF THE PATIENT LIVES ...

* CUPPING-GLASSES

BY AESCULAPIUS, THIS IS RIDICULOUS! A MAN WOULD REALLY HAVE TO BE AT DEATH'S DOOR BEFORE HE'D CONSULT A DOCTOR LIKE YOU!

WANT A SMACK IN THE AMPHORA THEN?

EXCUSE ME!

PEACE AND QUIET, THAT'S WHAT YOU NEED, PEACE AND QUIET!

LET ME SPEAK!

NEXT MORNING, IN THE VILLAGE...

YOUR MASTER'S ILL? HE NEEDS ME? I'M ON MY WAY!

ASTERIX! OBELIX! WE'RE OFF TO CONDATUM, AT ONCE! DROP EVERYTHING!

I AM ALWAYS BOUND TO HELP SICK PEOPLE, EVEN ROMANS

I DON'T LIKE ROMANS TO BE ILL. IT MAKES THEM SOFTER THAN USUAL

YOU MAY HAVE DIFFICULTY GETTING TO SEE MY MASTER

OBELIX AND I WILL SEE TO THAT. NO ROMAN EVER STOPPED US GETTING ANYWHERE YET!

DELIGHTED TO HEAR IT!

WELL, THAT'S THE FIRST TIME I EVER MET ONE OF YOU WHO WAS!

SOON AFTERWARDS, IN THE PALACE OF GOVERNOR VARIUS FLAVUS...

ZZZZZZZZZZZ WHEEEEEEE ZZZZZZZZ

SPLOSH!

?

SENTRY! WHY HAVE YOU LEFT YOUR POST? AND WHAT ARE YOU DOING IN MY COLD BOAR'S TRIPE FRIED IN AUROCHS DRIPPING?

I...GLUG!... I CAME TO WARN YOU THAT THREE GAULS HAVE BROKEN INTO THE PALACE. ONE OF THEM'S A DRUID

A DRUID?

HAS ANYONE GOT A SPOT OF HONEY?

YOU'RE ILL... VERY ILL. THE ONLY THING THAT MIGHT SAVE YOU IS A POTION OF WHICH I HAPPEN TO KNOW THE SECRET

MAKE IT, O DRUID! YOU WILL NOT FIND ME UNGRATEFUL

UNFORTUNATELY, AN ESSENTIAL INGREDIENT OF THIS POTION IS THE SILVER STAR *

SILVER STAR?

* EDELWEISS

A SMALL FLOWER WHICH GROWS ONLY ON THE HIGHEST MOUNTAINS... IT'S VERY DIFFICULT TO GET HOLD OF

GOOD, GOOD! I'LL SEND SOME OF MY MEN TO LOOK FOR IT!

BUT THEY'RE NOT WELL!

EXACTLY! THE MOUNTAIN AIR WILL DO THEM GOOD!

WHERE DO YOU HAVE TO GO TO FIND THIS WONDERFUL FLOWER?

HELVETIA, FOR PREFERENCE. THE BEST SPECIMENS FOR MY POTION GROW IN HELVETIA

DRUID, I HAVE COMPLETE CONFIDENCE IN YOU! SEND YOUR MEN IN SEARCH OF THIS SILVER STAR!

BUT WHY BRING FOREIGNERS INTO IT? LET'S KEEP THIS ROMAN!

ASTERIX, OBELIX, WOULD YOU MIND GOING TO HELVETIA?

NOT AT ALL. IT'S SOME TIME SINCE WE TOOK A TRIP ABROAD

AND YOU NEVER KNOW, WE MAY FIND ROMANS IN BETTER SHAPE ON THE MOUNTAINS THERE... I'M REALLY WORRIED ABOUT THE ONES WE HAVE HERE

WILL SOMEONE PLEASE LISTEN TO ME?

I MAKE JUST ONE CONDITION: YOU MUST STAY IN OUR VILLAGE AS A HOSTAGE UNTIL MY FRIENDS RETURN

NO, NO! NEVER!

VERY WELL, DRUID

AND I WARN YOU, IF MY FRIENDS DON'T COME BACK, THE HOSTAGE WILL BE EXECUTED!

WILL HE, THOUGH?

SINCE I HAVE NO ALTERNATIVE, I WILL GIVE ORDERS FOR YOUR DEPARTURE!

BUT WE DON'T USUALLY TAKE HOSTAGES, GETAFIX...

THIS MAN SINUSITUS HAS BEEN POISONED. IF HE STAYS HERE, I WOULDN'T GIVE TWO DENARII FOR HIS CHANCES OF SURVIVING. HE'LL BE SAFE FROM HIS WOULD-BE MURDERERS IN OUR VILLAGE

BUT I CAN'T KEEP HIM ALIVE VERY LONG! YOU MUST LEAVE AT ONCE, AND HURRY! I'LL SAY GOODBYE TO THE OTHERS FOR YOU

LOOK AFTER LITTLE DOGMATIX!

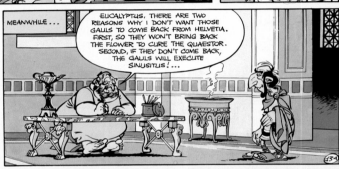

MEANWHILE...

EUCALYPTUS, THERE ARE TWO REASONS WHY I DON'T WANT THOSE GAULS TO COME BACK FROM HELVETIA. FIRST, SO THEY WON'T BRING BACK THE FLOWER TO CURE THE QUAESTOR. SECOND, IF THEY DON'T COME BACK, THE GAULS WILL EXECUTE SINUSITUS!...

SET OUT FOR GENAVA!* YOU WILL GIVE THIS MESSAGE TO GOVERNOR CURIUS ODUS. HE'S AN OLD FRIEND OF MINE. DON'T STOP ON THE WAY; I'LL GET THEM TO GIVE YOU A PACKED ORGY

* GENEVA

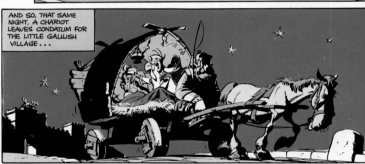

AND SO, THAT SAME NIGHT, A CHARIOT LEAVES CONDATUM FOR THE LITTLE GAULISH VILLAGE...

...A MESSENGER LEAVES FOR GENAVA...

... AND A GAULISH WARRIOR, ACCOMPANIED BY A MENHIR DELIVERY-MAN, GOES IN SEARCH OF A LITTLE FLOWER OVER THE HILLS AND FAR AWAY

THE NEW CHARIOTWAYS BUILT BY THE ROMANS ALLOW OUR FRIENDS TO TRAVEL FAST

WHAT DO YOU MEAN, YOU'RE HUNGRY? WE'VE ONLY JUST LEFT!

I ALWAYS FEEL HUNGRY WHEN I'M TRAVELLING!

I'VE GOT AN EMPTY HOLE INSIDE ME, JUST HERE

II MILIA PASSVVM

LOOK, OBELIX! WE CAN STOP TO EAT THERE

SERVITVTES

YES, IT'S VERY NICE. WITH LUCK, YOU'LL SEE SOME ACCIDENTS ON THE CHARIOTWAY WHILE YOU EAT...

MEANWHILE...

I SHOULDN'T HAVE HAD THAT COLD BEAR BLACK PUDDING...IT COULD BE INDIGESTIBLE... ANYWAY, AN ORGY'S NO FUN ON YOUR OWN

18

WHILE GOVERNOR VARIUS FLAVUS'S MESSENGER RIDES DESPERATELY ON, OUR FRIENDS ARE SPENDING THE NIGHT IN A NEW KIND OF INN WHICH HAS A STABLE TO EVERY ROOM . . .

CHARIOTEL

. . . AND IN THE PALACE OF GOVERNOR CURIUS ODUS, IN GENAVA, HELVETIA, AN ORGY IS JUST BEGINNING . . .

BRING ON THE CAULDRON OF MELTED CHEESE!

EVERYONE GOT IT ? IF YOU LOSE YOUR PIECE OF BREAD IN THE FONDUE, YOU PAY A FORFEIT! THE FIRST TIME IT'S FIVE OF THE BEST WITH A STICK; THE SECOND TIME YOU GET TWENTY LASHES WITH A WHIP; THE THIRD TIME YOU GET THROWN INTO THE LAKE WITH WEIGHTS TIED TO YOUR FEET !

WHAT AMUSING NOTIONS YOU DO HAVE, O DIVINE ODUS !

WE NEED THEM IN THIS STRAIT-LACED COUNTRY. I'VE TRIED HOLDING CIRCUSES, BUT THE WILD BEASTS WERE SO WELL FED THEY WOULDN'T EVEN TAKE A BITE OF THE PRISONERS !

AND AS FOR THEIR MANIA FOR CLEANLINESS!... AN ORGY IS SUPPOSED TO BE DIRTY!... STOP MOPPING THAT FLOOR, BY JUPITER !

OH DEAR ! I'VE LOST MY PIECE OF BREAD !

THE STICK! THE STICK !

HERE YOU ARE ! HERE YOU ARE !

OUR FRIENDS HAVE A FEW SETBACKS ON THEIR WAY, IN PARTICULAR A BROKEN WHEEL

IT'S READY

GOOD

CALL ME FAT! DID YOU SEE **HIS** SPARE TYRE?

WE'RE GETTING NEAR HELVETIA... LUCKILY, WE'VE LOST A LOT OF TIME

TOO MUCH TIME, IN FACT, FOR IN GENAVA...

MASTER, A VERY DIRTY MESSENGER HAS COME FROM VARIUS FLAVUS, ASKING TO SEE YOU, AND THERE'S A SPOT ON YOUR TUNIC JUST THERE!

NEVER MIND ABOUT MY SPOT. SEND HIM IN!

AVE!

HOW NICE TO SEE SOMEONE REALLY DIRTY! DRAW YOUR SWORD AND JOIN OUR ORGY!

LATER, O GOVERNOR CURIUS ODUS. I HAVE AN IMPORTANT MESSAGE FOR YOU!

CARRY ON WITHOUT ME, FRIENDS! HAVE FUN!

OH DEAR! I'VE LOST MY PIECE OF BREAD AGAIN!

THE WHIP!
THE WHIP!

BUT IT ISN'T DRY YET!

I CAN REFUSE NOTHING TO THAT OLD FRUIT FLAVUS, AND WHAT'S MORE, DISPOSING OF A QUAESTOR WILL BE A POSITIVE PLEASURE! I'LL GIVE ORDERS TO HAVE THESE GAULS STOPPED AT THE BORDER... NOW LET'S GET BACK TO THE ORGY

OH DEAR! I'VE LOST MY THIRD PIECE OF BREAD!

HARD CHEESE! INTO THE LAKE WITH WEIGHTS TIED TO HIS FEET!

WHAT BARBARIANS!

YES, THE WATER OF THE LAKE IS ALL MUDDY AT THIS TIME OF YEAR!

MEANWHILE...

HERE WE ARE, OBELIX!

GAUL ROMAN EMPIRE

HELVETIA ROMAN EMPIRE TOO

HALT! THIS IS A CHECKPOINT! YOU ARE NOW LEAVING GAUL!

WHAT DO WE DO, ASTERIX?

THESE ARE JUST THE FORMALITIES, OBELIX. WE HAVE TO GO THROUGH THEM

GAUL ROMAN EMPIRE

WHAT IS THE REASON FOR YOUR VISIT TO HELVETIA?

WE'VE COME IN SEARCH OF...

WE'VE COME IN SEARCH OF MOUNTAIN AIR

DECURION! A MESSENGER FROM GOVERNOR CURIUS ODUS. HE WANTS A WORD WITH YOU. IT'S URGENT

NO, NO, ASTERIX, THAT'S NOT WHAT WE'VE COME TO...

SHUT UP, OBELIX!

PSSSPSSSPSSSPSSSPSSS

AHA!

ALL RIGHT, GAULS! YOU CAN PASS!

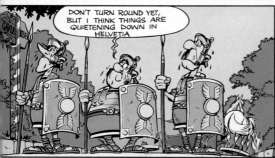

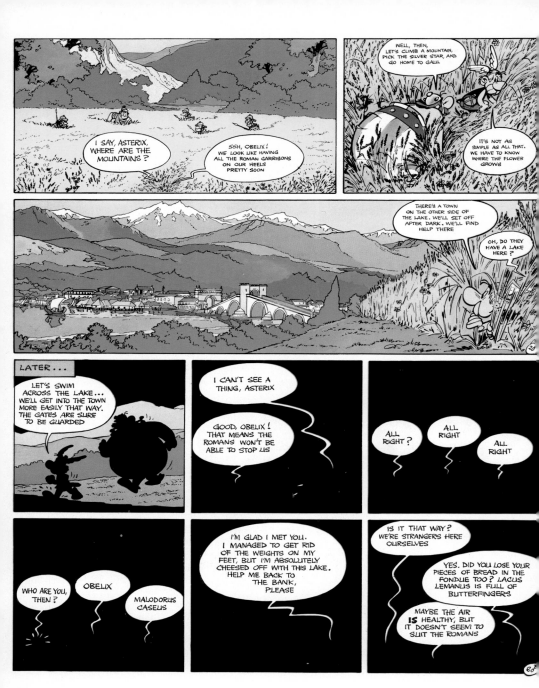

I SAY, ASTERIX, WHERE ARE THE MOUNTAINS?

SSH, OBELIX! WE LOOK LIKE HAVING ALL THE ROMAN GARRISONS ON OUR HEELS PRETTY SOON

WELL, THEN, LET'S CLIMB A MOUNTAIN, PICK THE SILVER STAR, AND GO HOME TO GAUL

IT'S NOT AS SIMPLE AS ALL THAT. WE HAVE TO KNOW WHERE THE FLOWER GROWS

THERE'S A TOWN ON THE OTHER SIDE OF THE LAKE. WE'LL SET OFF AFTER DARK. WE'LL FIND HELP THERE

OH, DO THEY HAVE A LAKE HERE?

LATER...

LET'S SWIM ACROSS THE LAKE... WE'LL GET INTO THE TOWN MORE EASILY THAT WAY. THE GATES ARE SURE TO BE GUARDED

I CAN'T SEE A THING, ASTERIX

GOOD, OBELIX! THAT MEANS THE ROMANS WON'T BE ABLE TO STOP US

ALL RIGHT?

ALL RIGHT

ALL RIGHT

WHO ARE YOU, THEN?

OBELIX

MALODORUS CASEUS

I'M GLAD I MET YOU. I MANAGED TO GET RID OF THE WEIGHTS ON MY FEET, BUT I'M ABSOLUTELY CHEESED OFF WITH THIS LAKE. HELP ME BACK TO THE BANK, PLEASE

IS IT THAT WAY? WE'RE STRANGERS HERE OURSELVES

YES. DID YOU LOSE YOUR PIECES OF BREAD IN THE FONDUE TOO? LACUS LEMANUS IS FULL OF BUTTERFINGERS

MAYBE THE AIR IS HEALTHY, BUT IT DOESN'T SEEM TO SUIT THE ROMANS

COULD YOU TELL US THE WAY TO A HOTEL, ROMAN?

THERE ARE HOTELS ALL ROUND THE LAKE. LOOK, THERE'S ONE RIGHT OPPOSITE

AND WHAT ARE YOU GOING TO DO?

GET SOME DRY CLOTHES ON AND GO BACK TO THE ORGY. WHAT FUN!

LAKESIDE HOTEL

WHAT'S A FONDUE, ASTERIX?

I EXPECT IT'S SOME KIND OF LOCAL ORGY

...YES, I HAVE GOT A ROOM FREE, EVEN THOUGH THEY'RE HOLDING THE ICTC— THE INTERNATIONAL CONFERENCE OF TRIBAL CHIEFTAINS — IN GENAVA JUST NOW

THERE WAS A BARBARIAN DELEGATION WHICH DIDN'T WANT THEIR ROOM. THEY SAID IT WAS TOO CLEAN

YOU MUST BE STRANGERS HERE... I'D BETTER TELL YOU, YOU SHOULD HAVE COME OVER THE BRIDGE. JULIUS CAESAR DESTROYED IT, BUT IT'S BEEN REBUILT NOW

MEANWHILE, IN THE GOVERNOR'S PALACE...

YOU BUNGLING IDIOTS! I MUST HAVE THOSE GAULS!

THE ROMANS ARE AFTER THESE TWO MEN. THEY'RE SEARCHING THE WHOLE TOWN. WE MUST SAVE THEM!

YES, OF COURSE. YOU HAVE OUR SYMPATHY. WE HAVE OFTEN FOUGHT AGAINST THE ROMANS, AND JULIUS CAESAR CONSIDERS US FORMIDABLE ENEMIES... BUT WHERE CAN WE HIDE YOU?

I HAD THOUGHT OF ONE OF YOUR SAFES, IN THE VAULT...

YOU'D HAVE TO OPEN AN ACCOUNT

WHAT, TO HIDE IN A SAFE?

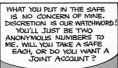

WHAT YOU PUT IN THE SAFE IS NO CONCERN OF MINE. DISCRETION IS OUR WATCHWORD! YOU'LL JUST BE TWO ANONYMOUS NUMBERS TO ME. WILL YOU TAKE A SAFE EACH, OR DO YOU WANT A JOINT ACCOUNT?

IF YOU HAVE A BIG ENOUGH SAFE, WE'D RATHER BE TOGETHER

THAT'LL BE QUITE IN ORDER. SIGN, PLEASE. THERE, THERE AND THERE

THIS WAY, PLEASE

HERE'S YOUR SAFE

CREEAK!

I'LL COME BACK TOMORROW. WE'LL KEEP YOU IN TOUCH

THANKS FOR EVERYTHING, PETITSUIX!

WAIT A MOMENT! THERE ARE NO REGULATIONS COVERING THE OPENING OF A SAFE FROM THE INSIDE. IF YOU WANT PETITSUIX TO COME AND OPEN IT, YOU MUST GIVE HIM A POWER OF ATTORNEY!

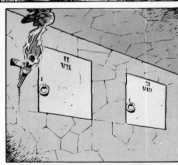

CUCKOO!

SHUT UP!

CUCKOO! WAKE UP, CHÉRI, HE SAID CUCKOO!

I SAY, WHAT A FEARFUL BORE!

AND YOU KNOW WHAT I SAY TO HIM...?

IF ONLY WE COULD TURN THESE HOURGLASSES OVER SEVERAL TIMES IN ADVANCE!

LAKESIDE HOTEL

HALF A CUCKOO LATER...

GET THEM OUT OF HERE! THEY'VE BROUGHT DISHONOUR ON MY NAME! THEY MADE ME LIE ABOUT THE SECURITY OF MY ESTABLISHMENT!

GOOD MORNING, ZURIX. I'VE COME FOR THE GAULS

I'VE HAD JUST ABOUT ENOUGH OF THESE GAULS!

CALM DOWN, ZURIX. THEY MADE ME DIRTY MY HOTEL

CLICK!

IT'S ENOUGH TO MAKE YOU WANT TO BECOME NEUTRAL

I'VE BROUGHT YOU DISGUISES. WITH THESE, YOU WON'T BE SPOTTED IN THE CROWD

THAT'S A DISGUISE??

CARRYING THOSE WEAPONS, YOU'LL LOOK LIKE HELVETIANS GOING TO THEIR ANNUAL CAMP. EVERY YEAR WE HAVE TO DO OUR MILITARY SERVICE FOR A NONES AND A CALENDS

ZURIX BAN

SLAM!

ALONE AT LAST! HOW GHASTLY, HAVING TO MIX WITH ALL THOSE FOREIGNERS, MY HORN RUNNETH OVER...

... AND I MUST SAY THAT I THINK WE CAN CO-EXIST WITH THE ROMANS. ALL WE NEED IS A LITTLE GOODWILL ON BOTH SIDES, AND RESPECT FOR INDIVIDUAL LIBERTY...

LET'S SPLIT UP. SIT DOWN AND IMITATE THE OTHERS!

OF COURSE, WE SHALL HAVE TO MAKE GREAT EFFORTS...

PRETEND TO BE ASLEEP

... BUT THE ROMANS HAVE ALREADY GIVEN AMPLE EVIDENCE OF THEIR DESIRE FOR PEACE...

ZZZZZZ

?!

PAX ROMANA! THAT COULD BE THE FORMULA FOR FUTURE PEACE, AND IF WE FORGET OLD HATREDS AND RESENTMENTS...

...I SEE BEFORE US A PERIOD OF UNTROUBLED CALM...

I SEE THE LITTLE TOUGH ONE!

FOLLOW ME!

COME ALONG, OBELIX!

...AND THAT IS WHY I SAY TO YOU...

OBELIX!

ZZZZZZ   ZZZZZZ

...THAT PEACE IS POSSIBLE...

CUCKOO!

...AND MUST BE POSSIBLE. THANK YOU FOR YOUR KIND ATTENTION

GET UNDRESSED!
KEEP YOUR WEAPONS!
JUMP TO IT! NUNC
EST BIBENDUM!

I'M FLOATING, OF
COURSE! THAT'S ALL I CAN
DO! I TRAINED FOR
THE INFANTRY,
DIDN'T I?

41

TCHAC!

CRUMP!

FIRST YOU HIT ME AND THEN YOU BANDAGE ME UP!

IT'S OUR VOCATION. WE LOOK AFTER ALL COMBATANTS, WHATEVER THEIR NATIONALITY...

AND WHILE THE BATTLE STILL RAGES...

LOOK OVER THERE! THE OUTLAWS ARE CLIMBING A MOUNTAIN! LET'S GET AFTER THEM WHILE THE OTHERS ARE BUSY HERE!

PAF!

BING!

WE GO SWIMMING IN THE LAKE, WE GO CLIMBING MOUNTAINS...

WHAT D'YOU EXPECT? WE'RE NOT ON HOLIDAY, YOU KNOW!

I'VE DONE IT! I'VE CAUGHT ONE!

45

the end

PRINTED IN BELGIUM BY
proost
INTERNATIONAL BOOK PRODUCTION